THE "FRENCH WRITERS OF CANADA" SERIES

The purpose of this series is to bring to English readers, for the first time, in a uniform and inexpensive format, a selection of outstanding and representative works of fiction by French authors in Canada. Individual titles in the series will range from the most modern work to the classic. Our editors have examined the entire repertory of French fiction in this country to ensure that each book that is selected will reflect important literary and social trends, in addition to having evident aesthetic value.

Current titles in the Series

(continued inside back cover)

Yves Thériault

Yves Thériault is the author of thirty books, a score or more of children's adventure stories, innumerable "dime" novels written during the forties under a pseudonym or anonymously, and over one thousand radio and T.V. scripts. His works encompass novellas, plays, short stories, and essays. His style ranges from the brutal realism of some of his earlier novels to the poetic prose of *Ashini*. The themes embrace eroticism, primitivism, and naturalism in varying degrees. His stories are set in the Canadian North, the city, the mountains, the plains, Canada, and Spain. Yet, they all reflect his sympathy with the "little people" who must fight against God, nature and society to survive.

Thériault once said, "I am interested in people who struggle to survive. Having lived in the Canadian wilderness for many years, having myself experienced harrowing poverty, I believe I understand the human condition when it is driven by bitter geography into a corner."

Not only does he understand and sympathize but, perhaps better than any other French Canadian author, he has been able to transmit this sense of desperation to the reader. He understand his characters, be they immigrant or native. Thériault himself is a non-conformist. Born in Quebec in 1915, of part Montagnais descent, and raised in Montreal, he is a self-taught man. He left school at the age of fifteen and embarked on a variety of occupations from cheese salesman to truck driver. A victim of tuberculosis, he spent a year in a sanitorium. When he got out, he began his career of radio announcing which lasted for five years. He has been a journalist, publicity manager of a war supplies factory, script writer for radio and the National Film Board, and for two years he was the cultural director of the Department of Indian Affairs in Ottawa. He travelled around the world in a freighter and spent some time in Italy and Yugoslavia. A member of the Royal Society of Canada, his works have won the PRIX DE LA PROVINCE DE QUÉBEC (twice), the PRIX FRANCE-CANADA (twice), and the GOVERNOR GENERAL'S LITERARY AWARD. In 1971, Thériault won the MOLSON PRIZE. One of his books has been translated into six languages. Thériault himself considers *Ashini*, a double prize winner, to be one of his best.

ASHINI

a novel by
YVES THÉRIAULT

translated by
Gwendolyn Moore

HARVEST HOUSE
Montreal

Advisory Editor

Ben-Zion Shek,
Department of French,
University of Toronto.

For information address Harvest House Ltd.
4795 St. Catherine St. W., Montreal,
Quebec H3Z 2B9

Printed and bound in Canada.
Designed by Sue Scott.

The Publishers gratefully acknowledge a
publication grant from The Canada Council.

ASHINI

Chapter One

When she was dead, I tied her skirt to her ankles. I attached her hands together, so that they would not dangle. Then, from the trunk of a nearby birch, I unwound long strips of bark in which I bound the limp and still warm body.

With my hands and my knife, I hollowed out the layer of needles and loose earth at the foot of a great pine.

A grave towards the west, so that my wife might voyage directly to the Land of Good Hunting.

On the trunk of the great pine, I inscribed the sign of repose.

The first of my sons sleeps at Lake Uishket-sa, drowned during a flash flood in the spring-time. A white man stinking of whiskey killed the other for me during a hunt. An accident.

My daughter fled the forest to serve the Whites, in town.

Now, my wife is dead, and I am alone.

Ashini, last of the blood of a great breed which came from the country to the south and made its home in the Ungava forest.

Last of my breed, because the others live at the mouths of the rivers, near the sea, held there by the hypocritical favours of the white man. Sold to the Whites for a mere pittance.

I, I am Ashini; the rock; the tenacious granite; the high stone at the heights of the bluffs, ravaged by the winds, polished by the chill rains.

Ashini, possibly the presiding spirit of this great domain.

Alone of this seed; alone in this servitude.

But alone.

I could wish to find tears.

Once more I followed the bear trails to regain the mountainous country between the Mécatina and the Goynish.

Twice I had returned to offer counsel; but the trail remained deserted behind me.

I travelled all that day until late in the evening; tired out, I rolled up in my blanket to sleep, without bothering to eat. At dawn, a loon called at the edge of the nearby lake; and then I ate a little, a few mouthfuls of bannock.

Am I really sixty years old? I am told that I was born in the year of the porcupines, which followed the time of the death of the trees with leaves. That must be sixty years ago; but I could not swear to it.

Have I lived?

Already my memories have become shrouded in mist. My daughter having scarcely departed, I found it difficult to remember her. (Nevertheless, she was strong and brown, as solid as the warm earth in July. That I know. Also her countenance, and her cries from across the lake as she summoned me from the farther shore. And her singing ... But her expressions? Her speech? ...)

My sons have also entered into the haze wherein I can distinguish nothing clearly. The eldest was true to our blood, as I am; tall, as I am, knowing in each of our sciences. As I am.

The other wanted to go down to Mingan or Betsiamits. That one believed in the white

11

man. So much that he was killed by the bullet of a white man.

(I will tell you how it happened. The White thought he saw a movement in the brush. His senses were frothy, as he had been drinking. He fired. He killed the man who was in the brush, examining a burrow. It was my son... my only remaining son...)

Then my wife.
Then the solitude.
Hourly I have had to discover the secret of solitude. How to live alone, eat alone, sleep alone, decide alone, travel alone...

Once back in the mountains, I searched for the trails. I was looking for game, rabbit or porcupine. (The porcupines have come back this year; there will be fisher, and the trapping will be good.)

I found only a few traces of summer mink, whose flesh is tough. Then a partridge hurtled from a thicket, and I killed it. I ate it on the spot, for I was pinched with hunger.

The sun was high, and marked the mid-day

In the glow of the summer noon, the forest was silent.

There were only the insects buzzing ceaselessly around me, harassing me to depart and to deliver their habitations from my presence.

When the sun declined, I left.

I had no destination in mind.

You see, only in this way did man, in the old times, learn so much from his ancient forests. He wandered alone and without destination. Then he took the time to stoop and study the bare living earth. He climbed the trees to watch the living sky. And if he heard the voices of animals or of the wind, of water and of trees, he listened until he knew them.

I think that, today, the good of man is his solitude, and that he loses all balance when he joins himself to other men.

Wait, that is not what I mean.

Certainly, I would wish for the return of my daughter, for the rebirth of my son, and for the awakening of my wife from her sombre grave. But I know today that my greatest thoughts have come only in solitude. When I had nothing else, no other person, nothing; only the frightening desire not to perish without having left a profound mark on this land of men.

Two months slipped by. Two months in which the only replies to my voice were the detonation of my rifle, the raucous cry of the nighthawk, the howling of the wolves or the roaring of a torrent ravaging the mountain side.

For two months I heard within myself, truly, only the beating of my heart, when tears came to me that I had no right to shed.

If there really is a Land of Good Hunting on the far side of the Greatest Lake; and if you of my blood live there, forefather and progeny, will you answer just once, this one time and nothing more, when I cry out in my desert . . . ?

Chapter Two

The evenings are now gripped in a dry and windy cold, and by morning the white frost covers the leaves and the barren ground.

Soon, the lakes will freeze, the ice will seal everything, and the first snows will come, hard and fine.

A night fire is needed now, and I sleep no longer in the open; instead, I huddle in the grottoes of the rocks and beneath the thickets.

In a little while, I shall have to build a shelter of balsam boughs and moss.

The fur will be prime by that time, and I shall be able to trap the animals, and exchange their pelts in the spring for my provisions.

Since I have been alone, I have met no one. The hinterland is my home. Further to the west and to the south are the great iron mines, the new towns and railroads, and along the shore of the Gulf -- the Côte Nord, as the white man calls it -- a civilization is growing.

The country I inhabit is still little known, frequented only by a few rare wanderers like myself, solitary men who are the bad wolves of the pack, the fugitives, the exiles.

But of these other companions of the open sky I had not encountered so much as the shadow for a long time. Neither Nascapi, the enemy of my people, nor Cree, nor Waswanipi, be it even the last surviving member of the former bands. Only my own echoes in this immensity.

Then, at the end of December, I met Kakatso. Or rather, one evening when I was sitting in front of my fire not thinking of anything, he arose before me out of the night of blue lakes and star-studded sky.

The night was insubstantial, borne in on the cold wind, or it arose, one might say, from the ground itself. In the distance, the familiar sound of night birds, a pack of wolves on the hunt, the irritable growling of an impatient bear.

I perceived no human sound, when suddenly before me stood Kakatso. He spoke before I could take aim and fire.

"Meltepeshkao!"

Indeed, it was a lovely evening. Words of understanding. The salutation which binds the tribal blood lines.

"Good."

I laid aside my rifle.

The man was a Montagnais. In the light of the fire, I could see the hair braided at his temples, the noble and placid countenance, and the impenetrable gaze. It seemed that his face was already familiar, that I had always known him.

Neither a Nascapi of mixed heritage, nor a thin and undernourished Cree, nor yet a Waswanipi with shifty eyes. This being from out of the cold night was, as I, a descendant of the great Abenaki breed. One who came from the south, a hunter of the rich forest.

He took his place on the other side of the fire, facing me.

I held out to him what was left of the freshly grilled rabbit, but he shook his head.

"I ate two valleys ago. I travel at night."

"And by day also?"

"Yes."

I waited for him to speak further, if he wished.

For a long time, he observed me, and I knew that his gaze was searching me as mine was searching him, and that he was learning as much of me as I was learning of him by this examination.

(Thus, that he was a solitary wanderer like myself, for a rip at the shoulder of his garment had been sewn together with cotton thread, the thread of the white man. If this man had a wife, she would have known how to mend it with fine babiche, chewed and drawn between the teeth, which makes the mended part stronger than the surrounding material. And that he was a trapper, like me, because the palms of his hands were discoloured by the musk glands of mink and marten. And that he had come from the south, for at his belt hung a rabbit skin still spotted with brown; to the south the fall season is later and the frost had not yet primed the pelts.)

"I am Kakatso," he said.

Kakatso, the Raven. A name which expressed well the fine, haughty countenance of the man, who was taller than I, and who resembled indeed a raven, perched, as he watched me. I had heard of him. He was a solitary trapper as I was.

"And I am Ashini," I said.

"The Rock," he murmured. "They have named you well."

I also am tall, and of larger build than most of my people, although smaller than Kakatso, the newcomer. My shoulders are solid and my arms muscular. And I have, besides, the endurance of a rock; I am a wall which one can sense, and upon which one's will can be completely broken.

I raised my hand, the palm open, and he did the same.

Then we fell once more into our silence.

He moved later when a gust of cold wind blew up from the lake and over the bare ground. The flames of the fire guttered, and Kakatso had murmured something which I was unable to hear.

Shortly, he repeated it.

"At the forks of the Mecatina, they were speaking of you."

(Joined at their source, and linked for half of their length, the Mecatinas divide four days before the coast. There is a campsite at the forks, a meeting-place for the wanderers of the Montagnais language.)

"I thought of going that way. Later, I didn't care to." They must have been talking about the death of my son.

"I have perhaps been looking for you," said Kakatso.

This was more than he had been going to admit.

"I am alone now," I said. "My sons are dead. My wife is dead."

He remained impenetrable, because among our people it is not the custom to show astonishment. The good manners of our race impose this immobility, this impassivity.

(This I tell you so that you may know everything about us. Now that I am far away, and inaccessible, where can you learn what is and what should be, what is not and should not be? Unless in this book of blood. You are probably a white man, who believes he knows it all, and has never learned the only science that matters, that of living.)

"Where did she die?"

"At Lake N'tsuk."

"A woman is lithe, is industrious and gay,

like the otter," said Kakatso. "It is fitting that your wife died at Otter Lake."

"Yes," I said.

The air was suddenly still, and the smoke mounted from the fire, twisted in a curling spiral. Black, against the profound blue of the sky, against the path of the new moon which bridged the lake up to our camp.

A tardy insect, the last before the freeze-up, buzzed in the moss beside me. I searched for it with my hand to crush it, but withheld the gesture. Why should it die, if I were to live? Could it not build itself some cocoon wherein it could nestle and await the renewal of spring?

There would be no renewal for me. Only the last, stumbling steps to be accomplished in a year, or in ten years. Finally, to succumb on some lonely mountainside.

To die, watching the trees.

And to die, absorbed in the sky.

And to bequeath my body of fresh meat to the fur-bearing animals, who would draw from it a reprieve, so that a man younger than myself, my successor in the solitude, would trap them at a propitious time, and himself gain a reprieve.

The slow, cyclic mechanism of nature. Will you change even one of its impulses?

Will you modify its course?

It is to the Land of Good Hunting that the golden-hearted and wise hunters go, there to become the Gods, the Manitous, the regents and masters of all things around us, the teachers of us who obey them. Only they could change the course of the stars and the growth of the vegetation.

But they have forgotten me for such a long time; or perhaps the old gods no longer rule this wild country...

Could the white man, who has invented a god, conceive of the supreme Tshe Manitou, so great that he is above even my own gods, the humble gods who are content with the wilderness, and who are ignorant of the government of a metropolis?

Or else, rather than a Tshe Manitou who is strong in his justice, an evil spirit of great power capable of governing all, even the towns, even the airplanes, even the white man

22

stinking of whiskey and, even more, the solitary wanderers like myself and their Manitous without glory?

I want to believe in something, and I find nothing greater than any other, far above all things, unfailing and supreme.

I do not know how to invent new gods.

"What will you do now?" asked Kakatso.

(And I understood that he had searched for me with the sole aim of helping me if I needed it. Is it not in this way that we form our strongest ties with one another, the men of our great race? By not leaving our brother to despair in vain. Kakatso had not even known that my wife was dead. Only that my last living son had perished by drowning.)

"I have the whole country to travel," I said. "I shall go on."

(To go on, that is the logical aim. For him who knows how to get up again and to continue the journey, the tempest becomes merciful, the cold less mortal, the pain less relentless, destiny more kind. From falling, certainly, no one is exempt! Then, to get up again and to journey on.)

"I shall do as I have always done."

My gesture took in the entire country.

"There is fresh meat for food, the forest to shelter me, fur to trap and pure air to breathe."

And mountains to contemplate and the stars to admire, and the cold November moon to invoke, and all the beautiful and the good which envelops us and sustains us — the fragrance of the wind, the fresh scent of the white water, the incense of the pines, and the music of all the sounds of this region.

Why would anyone ever want to leave it, or to look for another country? What region could one find more majestic, greener, more health-giving?

"You will go on," said Kakatso. "That is good."

He, who wandered alone as I did, knew that he would be a coward to leave it all.

Following upon this thought, he said to me: "Tiernish is now alone; he has gone down to Betsiamits, where he will live on the reserve with his sister. Pikal also is going to Betsiamits, now that his son is studying the knowledge of the white man in the town. That will make two less of us."

Two cowards.

Pikal, an odd, sickly, little man, who had never really known how to find his way in the woods, as if there flowed in his veins some of the inferior blood of the ignorant White.

Tiernish, a better man, but one who built cabins of logs rather than temporary shelters, and who completely cleaned out the game in his district, being too lazy to travel over the portages, a task that he considered useless.

At the reserve, they would smother him with attention — the last deserter they would find to celebrate. He would be given food, money, shelter, and they would make an example of him to the children.

"Do you see that man over there? He is a sensible one; he is intelligent. He does not keep on living miserably in the woods. He comes here, where the white man will be good to him. Come, little ones, learn French, forget your language, distrust the forest; we offer you paradise on earth. We offer — it's beyond belief — to make white men of you! Is this not the very height of understanding and generosity?"

Tiernish, Pikal, two more down there, two less up here. The forest empty, become once more the land of silence, the realm of the relentless ones like me, like Kakatso, like Misesho, like Uapistan, the last of the free. Are there now twelve of us, or twenty?

I would not know.

There have been so many cowards, so many traitors, so many deserters...

The howl of a wolf — a symbolic cry. He also has been driven out, driven back towards the stunted trees of the far North, rejected, shamed, banished.

Like me; like us.

"Come, little one, let us make a white man of you..."

Afterwards, Kakatso slept, and I also, the two of us encircling the fire, until the chill dews of the autumn dawn.

We each took our separate ways, opposite but similar, and at noon that day I was alone again, more alone than I could ever have imagined, because there were two men less to cross the trails that I might travel.

Whether in the high ranges or in the tortuous valleys, such men as I who keep faith with the trails do not fear solitude, if they have known nothing else.

It is to have lost what one has known that tears from a man the last shred of his joy. There is no art more simple than that of walking alone upon a path.

But there is no art more difficult than to walk alone upon the path that one has formerly travelled with others.

Therein is the origin of my malady, the grievous root of my pain; what cry could I sound forth, that I might be answered?

My open eyes saw only a land void of my people. My nostrils perceived no odours of home. My hands touched only the silent echoes thrown back by the winds, swirling without direction.

And for my consolation only one escape, that of turning inward towards my memories. But why, then, do I find there only the agonies of my wife, slow, restless, and cruel? And not our former life of love?

Why could I not relive those peaceful dialogues at the borders of the evenings with that one of my sons whom the drunken White had slaughtered? And why could I see only, in each evocation, the violet hole in the brown back, and the blood on the green leaves?

As for my daughter — only the image of her flight when she left us without returning, and without hearing my lament?

Seated in the red moss of June, I imagined once more the drowning of my son. I had examined the place of his death. By the signs, I had long ago reconstructed all the stages.

Why could I not recall our hunts together, silent and yet eloquent? Both of us equally slender and tall, equally adept, when we were tracking a caribou and knew that we would dine on the fresh meat that very night?

The cry of the caribou borne in on the wind from the valley, a cry both futile and despairing. The same cry as my own, desolate and voiceless, which I sent forth this day on remembering this elder son who was to have been the fulfilment of my honour and the very nourishment of my self-esteem...

That evening, the night before his death by drowning, my son Antoine Ashini made a fire, dismembered a hare which he had killed during the day, and prepared it for his evening meal. Afterwards, he slept. But, at midnight, the temperature changed abruptly. From the brisk cold of the day, it climbed rapidly to a menacing thaw.

At dawn, the snow melted, and water flowed everywhere through the ground. All at once, the ice of the falls gave way, and the torrent roared down from the heights. An enormous mass of water surged over the low-lying areas. Antoine awakened, tried to escape; but he was too late. The flood reached him, and he was swept away towards the lake. Now followed a combat such as he had never before endured: with his entire strength, and more by instinct than by design, he attempted to resist this great force which charioted him along like a straw. Fighting, he thrashed with his arms and legs, and clung to every projection in his passage. But the water was the stronger. Beaten, bruised, he was drawn into the lake. And suddenly, he found himself in darkness. A terrible pressure gripped his chest. He was swallowing water, suffocating, and the more he struggled, the more he was restrained by something, a solid layer, a ceiling which was holding him in, and which entrapped him.

Suddenly, he understood. The torrent had swept him into the lake and had projected him beneath the ice. To save himself, he must act immediately. He thought of finding a spot where the ice had been broken, but renounced the idea at once. He did not know in what direction to go. If he were mistaken, he risked going even further into the lake, and that meant certain death. These ideas tore through his brain like forks of lightning.

He reasoned immediately that the ice on the lake was not thick enough to support a man. Drawing his knife from its sheath, and pushing against the surface above him with his other hand, he struck at the ice with forceful blows. But he scarcely scratched the obstacle. A pressure against his thigh reminded him that he had gone to sleep with his hatchet stuck in its holder. With a rapid gesture, he let fall the useless knife, which drifted to the bottom of the lake.

With the new tool, he had better results. The ice gave way, little by little. His lungs were almost bursting, and his head pounded. First he chopped out a hole as large as his hand, then large enough to put his head through. Quickly, he breathed through the hole. He was saved. He plunged back, and, as he was a good swimmer, he had no difficulty in enlarging the hole to a practicable size. But one problem remained, that the ice was too thin to bear him. All the same, he succeeded in pulling himself out of the water. Then, stretched out at full length, he slid along the unstable surface without causing as much as a tremor; in this way he was able to bring himself almost to the edge... There, the water was not very deep; he stood up and ended the voyage breaking through the weakened ice with high, smashing strides, and reached the sandy shore.

He reached it, exhausted, let himself go, and lost consciounesss.

But the temperature changed again. The thaw was followed by a biting cold. When Antoine awoke, he was benumbed, and a shiver shook his entire body. Painfully, he managed to drag himself as far as the bivouac of the previous night. Some dry wood remained where he had cached it under the brush. Quickly he lit a match to dispel the cold, which was overcoming him. But his hands were trembling so much that he wasted nearly all the matches in the waterproof match case before succeeding in getting the wood to light.

Hugging the new fire, he tried to warm himself. But in vain he piled on the dry twigs, in vain he sought to get even closer to the heat. He still trembled convulsively, and his teeth chattered in his mouth. He should have removed his wet clothing, but he had no other clothing to put on. Half dead, he dragged himself on all fours over to his supply of dry wood. But the fire, although more lively, brought no relief. He felt his head become feverish, and his respiration difficult. Soon his breath was rasping. And then, laid low, he curled up around the fire and lost consciousness once more.

In his sleep he cried out; he became delirious, and his remaining hours were terrible. But no one heard his cries, nor his thrashing about. Finally the fire died and only the cold remained, a fatal burden, crushing Antoine.

We found him two days later. In death, his face was twisted as if possessed by an evil spirit.

Chapter Three

The year of my birth, the porcupines, which had vanished from the region five years before, returned, and there was an influx of black mink. In these events, my father read an augury.

When I was twelve years old and had taken my first caribou, he said, "You were sent among us to bring us good hunting."

I knew before long that I was not the issue of any god, because I suffered from the cold like the others, and when I was wounded the blood flowed red, and not pure white as does the blood of the Manitou.

And if at one time I was filled with pride at my alleged spiritual lineage, I was soon disenchanted. I too, a Montagnais like the others, was held in submission by the Whites.

But within the confines of a forest which was now surveyed and cadastered, I believed myself free, as long as my servitude was masked by a false portent.

I was on the verge of manhood when I learned the truth.

My father, while instructing me, said one day: "When you go hunting, you must not travel where Mont Uapeleo (the Mountain of the White Partridge) stands out above the Greatest Lake. Beyond that mountain lies the Land of Good Hunting, where only the elect among the dead may go. To the west of the lake is the land of the white man, where the salmon in the rivers are forbidden to the people of our race, where the fur in the bush belongs only to the Whites, and where, if you hunt, you will no longer be an Indian. Do you want to be a white man?"

I, become a white man?

I, Ashini, as enduring as the stone, the son of Uapekelo, the White Owl, which can glide over the forest like a summer cloud?

Beyond these frontiers, then (and there remained to us all the same as much territory as the largest of countries in which we could travel as the masters) I dealt with the white man only when we traded. Unhappy encounters from which I always emerged humiliated, frustrated and deceived.

But I shall not make of these the subject of this book, the only one which will ever be written about my vanishing race, of whose existence and of whose dignity no one even knows any more.

I grew up free, but my liberty was that of a bird in a cage. There are cages which are aviaries, where a bird can cherish the illusion of open sky and illimitable flight. There are also cages which are as narrow as prisons.

I lived in the great cage, an immense aviary for the free falcon that I was. But I felt free only by lying to myself. Would I have been able, at my will, to paddle my canoe from the delta of the Natashquouanne as far as the upper reaches of the river, to kill fresh meat and catch fish at will, and to come ashore at whatever spot I pleased?

Or rather would I find all along the banks of this river, which was formerly our royal way, the towns of the white man, the laws of the white man, the fences and the constraints of the white man? Along the course of this river, would I still be as a king visiting his kingdom?

At each bend of the river, at each chance encounter, at each necessary kill, would I not hear the cry which we now know so well:
"Get out, you damned savage!"

There are pure languages which have been deformed by colonial usage. I can appreciate how this may have happened. To the far-away people of the mother tongue, who made of the language a sweetness and a joy, belongs a gentle heart and a serene sympathy.

To the usurper and the intolerant, the vulgarity of a tongue corrupted and made ugly.

"Get out, you damned savage!"

There is no gentle tongue which could pronounce such words against a people who have maintained, for thousands of years, the image of man before the instinctual forces of nature, who have travelled these forests as beneficent masters, without ever decimating the animal life, without ever setting fire to the trees, without ever polluting the watersheds. Good masters, adapted to nature, who would not dream of disturbing its rhythms.

In my language, as astonishing as it might seem, there are no words in which one can cry out to the intruder, "Get out, you damned white man!" Perhaps we should have invented these words before it was too late?

I did not invent them, nor my brothers; my sons, even less.

We lived, then, in our immense cage, circumscribed, but imagining ourselves to be free.

And my life was as that of my people. I drew my livelihood from the forest, there I took a wife, and there I fathered children: and we were nomads, following the migrations of the animals, following the spring floods, subject to the whim of the winds, of the snow, and of the sun, each of us to attain finally our allotted end.

Chapter Four

Could I truthfully say at what moment the Great Thought came to me?

I can recognize only the influence of my solitude, which from that time forth plunged me within myself for human companionship.

Alone on my trails, far from all human discourse, I had only myself to interrogate, and only my own replies to hear.

Did it come to me when I felt myself engaged in an enterprise that was futile, that of living alone from then on? What was I, and of what use was I? Certainly, I had already accomplished my work in life. I had taken a wife, I had brought children into the world. But I still had the strength of a man.

I was still a human animal. My muscles were as strong and my body as lithe as they had been when I was twenty. My age was only a number.

But I had no taste for starting all that over again; and know this, I had no inclination at all to seek out some group where I might find a woman desirous of sharing my future.

I had already done those things which had to be done, according to the normal design of life, and I did not intend to start doing them over again.

Nevertheless, the fact that I was not committed to some useful work gripped me with a dull pain. I killed to feed myself; I trapped according to my needs. I travelled — from lake-head to outlet, from the lowlands of a river to the source, from the mouth of a stream to its precipitous origins, with no goal other than that of constant movement, of displacement without distinct purpose.

Now that I was free, I seemed to be frequented by beings who until now had been silent — my other selves, in some way, long unrecognized, who impelled me to accomplish something that I could not quite grasp.

And suddenly, one evening, it all came to me in a flash.

It was already November. For almost a month winter had lain over the forest. The lakes had frozen solid, and the calm stretches of the rivers were encased in ice; the crests of the rapids seemed slower and more viscous.

The undergrowth was thick with snow, and the young balsams heavy with their white burden, which bowed down their branches.

I was now warm when I slept, because I could burrow into the insulating mass of a snowbank and weave there a low shelter of branches; here, my fire threw its full heat.

Now was the time of good living in the woods, even more than in the autumn or in the spring, when the air is heavy with dampness.

It was no longer necessary to search for the trails of the animals to be trapped; these showed up clearly in the snow. And the famished beasts could be caught without ruse and without effort.

Was it the fruit of solitude, on that evening, that I could allow myself to perceive, with full clarity, the Great Thought, which suddenly and distinctly arose within me?

Under my shelter, heated by a lively and sparkling fire, I was watching the black night and the white snow. The cold had moderated outside, and the trees were silent.

The whole world seemed to be embalmed, and it was hard to imagine that, beyond the horizon, there existed immense cities, a whole country in servitude to the white man, a country violated by concrete roads and buffeted by the machinery of 'progress.'

Here, only the silence of nature, and in the sky an immensity of stars.

My country, the land of the Montagnais.

Of the Montagnais?

Since this Ungava, this Labrador, this Côte Nord, this peninsula as immense as a kingdom in itself, belonged really to the Whites, who had already begun to use it as they wished, pushing us nomads back as far as the Pentecôte River, beyond the Outardes River, and further still; since it was no longer the land of the Montagnais (that was an illusion that I had entertained about it) — why should not I be its liberator?

The creator of a new destiny for my people?

Had there as yet been any one of us who

had claimed, in all honour and dignity, the right of the Montagnais to live according to their own custom?

That night I did not sleep at all. I ransacked every recess of my memory. I examined all my recollections. Had I ever heard of anyone, among my contemporaries or among my elders, of even one of us, who had gone to place our cause before the white man?

I could name almost every Montagnais living in Ungava. I knew the history of each one of those who remained in the forest, and that of almost all the others who were agonizing on the reserves. Who among them had ever defended our rights, our heritage?

(On those occasions when I have visited the coast and the white villages when the white man was busy with politics, how often have I heard him deliver his discourses about HIS patrimony, HIS language, HIS traditions, about the roots which HE has plunged into the shores of the St. Lawrence, the Father of Waters... But nothing that concerns OUR heritage, thousands of years old, which he does not even recognize.)

This Thought worked deep within me, installed itself, acclimatized itself.

No recollection of any of us having gone before the tribunals of their land for the repatriation of our privileges.

Not one deed accomplished, not one leader to lead such a struggle.

I alone.

And then in the form of a question. I alone ? Was this, then the work which destiny proposed to me ?

An enterprise of the Tshe Manitou, perhaps, coming from the silences which surrounded me, to trace a path for my wanderings ?

My resolution was made that winter night on the shores of Lake Ouinokapau. I would undertake the long voyage to the reserves. I would go to present my cause, and that of my people.

Exaltation overwhelmed me, an immense joy, the presentiment of all these miracles accomplished. I would obtain from the Whites the concession of the entire region between Lake Attikonak and the Hamilton Falls. This would be enough certainly for all of my people!

Then, like the Messiah of whom the white man speaks, I would go to preach in the villages, on the reserves, and to every group of turncoats among my people. I would show them this country, free and indeed their own, untouchable in perpetuity by any other than the descendants of the great Abenaki race.

I would lead whole families back into these regions, and they would finally inhabit every turn of the valleys, every point of the lakes, and the banks of every river where fragrant flowers grow.

In the country which I had liberated and which would be our own, the song of humanity would rise everywhere.

Let the white man inhabit the low-lying part of the country from one end to the other. Let them have the rugged coasts, the luxuriant plains, the hardwood forests! In our forests, pure and remote, we would be the masters. No one could come to plunder the minerals or disrupt the flow of the waters. The game of riverbank and thicket, the trees, and even the smallest and most beautiful wildflower would be our heritage.

There would be no tender herb, no bayberry, no healing root that would not be for our own enrichment.

The bird in the sky and the insect, the animal and the fish, the black spruce and the gentle water lily, the wild thyme and the juniper would be ours, as would each stone, each drop of water, each breath of wind, each pearl of dew.

And the incontestable right to keep all of it until the end of time.

As for myself, I wished for nothing more than to wander at will, repatriated in my own land.

And for my people, I wished the reestablishment of our race and the return of our pride.

Was this, then, the proposal of a madman ?

I did not know at that time that the law of the Just Ones had not yet been voted for in the civilized countries of the earth.

It is only we, the primitives, the savages of the world, who can dispense equity of judgment.

In this ability lies, perhaps, the greatest of our anachronisms...

Chapter Five

I did not concern myself at that time with the eventual methods of defending my cause. Was it necessary to prepare a statement, to enumerate balanced arguments, or to compile a brief?

I was asking only that the lands which had been stolen from us be returned to us. I was not asking for the whole country, for this would be an illogical although just claim; not the colonized soils, but my forest, which should be for all of us, a country where no white man had as yet come to look for riches.

A country, in short, which was completely uninhabited, and which was of no use to anyone, but which could be of use to my people.

Such a small part of the map.

Why would I not have wished to present my demands to the highest authority? To the Great White Chief himself? With him alone would I agree to talk.

For, in proclaiming the rights of an entire people, I would become the equal of a chief. I did not want to be honoured, and I would never accept the chieftainship of the re-established tribes. But at the time of the conferences I would be chief, and therefore I would have the right to deal with a chief.

I knew the name of the white chief, his status, and where he lived on the banks of the former Ouataouas, the river which in ancient times brought the Mohawk people back home from their hunting expeditions in the north country.

It was the Great White Chief whom I would confront. He alone could authorize the recognition of my demands.

I did not even imagine a language barrier. I knew that among the Whites there were interpreters capable of translating our words so that the white man could grasp our ideas.

And, in contrast to the impoverished language of the Whites, I offered the richness of my Montagnais language.

A language that is rhythmic, ardent, rustling, like the wind in the leaves.

And, as did even the most humble of my people, I possessed within my being all the richness of this language, learned, furthermore, without a teacher, for it is in accord with the simplicity of things.

And these things are in themselves so varied, so beautiful, so magical, that the words that name them become a music and an ecstasy.

Shall I tell you what this language is like?

Look at the mountain. It is called 'otso'...
But spoken while drawing the breath, the sounds hardly uttered, the lips half-closed.

And if the mountain (otso) is linked with other mountains and becomes a chain, it is 'nattekam.' You see — a word for each thing, and for each thing a different word, one word only, and not the conjoining of words into laboured phrases characteristic of your depleted language.

The sand, 'leko;' and, in the water, this emerging rock, 'tshissekats;' but for an ordinary rock, such as protrudes in a clearing, 'ashini,' the rock, my own name.

The water in the brook, 'shipis,' and the white water of the rapid, 'paoshtuk.' The waves of the lake, the blue and limpid water, 'emikaits.' Misty days are called 'keshkum,' and when the storm is over and a rainbow is arched into the sky, 'uikuelepeshaken.' And if the rainbow reaches from one horizon to the other, 'lekepeshaken sheneteo.'

I could teach you words in this way for a long time, and show you that if you want to speak of a heart, in your language, and to whom it belongs — heart of a deer, heart of a fox, heart of a man, heart of an owl, I have in my language a separate word for each one of these hearts, and often two words for them, one to express the objective reality and one to express the inner nature of a thing, each in its own way.

There is a consonance between the words and our daily lives, but because our lives are experienced in a rich and noble immensity, our words have grandeur.

This is why I can tell my story in a way that surprises the ignorant, who will not admit that I can do so in words more noble than their own.

In my language, I repeat, I could express a hundred times more than the Great Chief could reply in his cold and arid English.

Therefore, I was better armed than one would have thought when I set out for the shores of the sea, for Betsiamits, where I hoped to find ears to hear me.

I journeyed for some time along the Pikapac River, where there are many portages. Then I travelled overland, following the escarpment, and reached the headwaters of the Manicouagan. Descending to the shores of the sea, I cached my canoe and went on foot to Betsiamits, skirting the villages of the white man through the borders of the woods.

At Betsiamits, I sought Pikal, and found him.

Skinny little Pikal, a vessel of bitterness, his face gaunt, his eyes blind to the beauty of things. (This was, I believe, the malady which made him abandon the only regions suitable to our race and return to this village on the reserve.)

He welcomed me into his house, for he possessed a house now, like the most ordinary of the Whites. A joyless structure, lifeless and miserable, topped with a peaked roof.

The doorstep was worn away by a thousand entries and exits, the toll of thirty years of use. How many among those who had entered here would rather have proudly stalked the open ground than have inhabited this undignified shack, this emblem of servitude? Whosoever had passed voluntarily through this door, had he not entered a prison organized by the Whites?

"You will have homes . . ."

And so the crowd came running. Should I blame my people? A little, because they entered these confines without being forced; at least, not by armed power. No one holds them at the end of a knotted chain. No one brandishes a gun. And the shepherds of the flock smile.

Because the white man has arms that are worse than guns. One can defend oneself against a gun. One can avoid being taken in chains with steel links. One can reply to force with force.

51

What can one do when words are pronounced which are themselves arms — promises, assurances, images that are made to
sparkle?

"You will have homes and streets. You will
elect a tribal council, and you will govern
yourselves. You will be given a territory on
which to hunt as you wish, and which will
be forbidden to the Whites. You will be your
own masters, and nothing will be imposed on
you, provided that you agree to sign here,
at the bottom of this treaty of agreement..."

Then those of my race who were short-
sighted placed the cross of their ignorance
at the bottom of the parchment.

What were they being given, and what were
they being asked to sacrifice?

To the white man, they ceded their most
fertile soils, their richest game forests, the
greater part of their country. They abandoned
all their rights, and were no longer able even
to vote at the conferences of the Whites.

And what did they receive in return? Some
homes, so-called. But I know of shelters made
of boughs that are palaces in comparison,

and from whose open flanks I can gaze upon the untouched mountains and the free waters...

And I know such shelters to be simple and useful objects, dismantled at dawn and set up again a day's journey further, there, where even now there are waters that are free, and high mountains...

From the doors of their houses, what do these people of the reserves see? If not a poverty similar to their own? If not rags such as they have? If not the squalour of degeneration, and the rickety forms of their undernourished children?

But, beneath these caps of roofs, does there not sleep each night the hope of a new dawn? Or is there only the knowledge of tomorrows similar and sad, equally monotonous, sterile and vain, enduring from one generation to the next, until the race, corrupted by the schools, will have forgotten all their ancient knowledge, and will have become, without choosing, false white men forever?

They do not even keep their language, that rhythmic and magnificent consolation, which would be for them a kind of raft, or a torch in the darkness. Their own language is disappearing, to be replaced by that of the Whites.

You whose skin is red, will you find a place in the cities of the white man? Or will you be rejected because of your colour, as in other countries the white man rejects the black, the yellow and the brown?

What have you received from the white man, for having given him everything?

When they did not even assure you, on their parchments, of the air that you bequeath your descendants, of the sunlight which will warm you, or of the waters which are to be yours?

Or — this brings a smile — do you imagine you will spend even one whole day playing the free man in the quarters of the rich Whites?

Can you show white paws, whose palms are not marked forever by the blood of your race? Is there some pigment which will colour your skin white, even if you spoke all the phrases of the fashionable world, and walked like an Englishman upon their cement sidewalks?

Pikal had little to say to me.

We had never really been blood brothers. Formerly, when we met in the forest, we did not know how to talk to each other, and found little to say, except to discuss the weather foreshadowed by the sky, or the price of fur.

In his house, he offered me a seat, and we smoked together.

He imparted to me only one valuable piece of information. With it I would have to content myself. At Betsiamits, the most pampered of the reserves of the Côte Nord, a new superintendent had taken up residence.

"This one," said Pikal, "likes the Indians. He will do everything for them."

"Everything?"

"That is what he said."

I returned to the forest that evening and slept in a shelter beside a stream. I had to weigh what I was going to say to this new man. My thoughts appeared to be no longer in the same terms as those which had come to me in the North. What would be the outcome of my auguries?

This incertitude was because I had, in my turn, observed the life of the reserve through the open door of the house of Pikal. I had seen its hopelessness, but I had seen also that the people appeared to be bound to it.

And the vacancy of their expression?

If I showed them the free country far to the north, would that be enough for them to follow in files along my trails?

But during the night, when a great wind whistled down out of the North, cold as a stream of living ice, there came into my dreams the greatest of the Montagnais of legendary times, nameless, but of the race of heroes honoured in our songs.

I saw him fall like a stricken tree, tumble down the side of the mountain, and disappear into a black abyss.

I think that I understood from that moment what I would have to do in order to gather around me all the amorphous lives, the deserters, and the cowards. I would have to commit an act that would stir whatever was left of their pride.

(When the great Abenaki race faced its enemies in ancient times, there were long combats which endured for many seasons. But the enemy was powerful. They possessed the sciences of the lands south of the horizon, where the sun stands overhead at noon. The warriors of my tribe were pushed back. Those who fled north of the Father of Waters were the vanquished, but they were not cowards. They found in Ungava the silence, the serenity, and the fresh meat to sustain the tribe. Who can blame them for not having reconquered their former lands, which had been inhabited by others since that time? They were wise, not cowards; they began a new life, so that those who preceded me could be born, so that I in my turn could be born. All that I asked was that this bloodline perpetuate itself forever in this same country which had permitted it to survive. Was this too much to ask...?)

In the morning I went back to the reserve. I crossed the paved road, where some enormous trucks were transporting rock. What other disembowelment of my soil had the Whites devised? They had built a town — Sept Isles — and had forced the Montagnais of that calm bay to evacuate and to resettle by the Moisie River.

There was talk of constructing a port, which was to be named Port Cartier, where formerly had been only a great shelf of rock. (Cartier — wasn't that the name of the White who was the first to come here, and who cajoled my ancestors by promising them a god and a king?)

Everywhere along this Côte Nord now, the Whites shattered the granite, pushed back the forest, and mutilated the mountains. To obtain iron or copper ore, to harness the rivers and conduct electricity to the demanding monsters of the country to the south, what would they not do?

And still, in their prideful recitals of their exploits, do they not neglect to mention that all these enterprises are just ant hills? That these laborious excavations do not equal the amount of soil washed down in the spring by even a single river of Ungava? That from the altitude of the gods, these new towns, mines, roads and dams are not even visible?

And what remained of my sole strength, of the great forest lands that lay still untouched?

Build your towns!

Ape the gods!

Play your games of geographical reconstruction!

There still remains enough territory in which to lose my entire nation, and in which to release them forever from all bondage.

It was easy for me to find the house of the white man. It was new and bright, whereas the houses of the Montagnais were grey and dirty.

"I know who you are," he told me, when I presented myself.

He looked at me curiously. It would be easy to talk to him because he would listen to me.

"I have come," I said, "because I want my people to be free."

Chapter Six

Advantages, concessions and promises are inscribed on the treaties. And other things too.

Meeting in council, the Whites, who wished to neutralize the Indian forces of Canada, designed a policy by which the redskin would be given just enough, and there would be taken from him very precisely what was necessary, for the colony to be explored and exploited forever without concern.

They marked off territories for us, never the best, but which were accepted by some of the chiefs of our tribes as being the magnanimous gift of the victors.

They tolerated the election of councils, and in certain tribes they permitted the perpetuation of the maternal line of descent.

On their maps, they inscribed the hunting territories reserved for my people. Whether they were Montagnais or Cree, Blackfoot or Shoshone, whether they inhabited the plains, the coniferous forests, or the escarpmented heights of the Rockies, each received a share, a lot fell to each.

But for those of us who had dreamt of a land of our own, which would be ours in all freedom, the reality of these treaties was atrocious.

It was an open and common serfdom which was formulated for our lives. We were the slaves of new masters, who did not exact labour, but who bound in servitude the entire future character of our racial destiny.

Then time flowed on, and the people of our blood perished on the reserves, because the promises were not kept and the agreements were forgotten.

Here and there, by instinct of survival, a tribe prospered. (Mine was less miserable than that of the Oskelanos, less pitiable than that of the Nascapi.)

Elected chiefs were permitted, and these met in councils as serious as any in the world, to vote on resolutions which the distant Whites in Ottawa, ignoring the welfare of our people, refused to ratify.

I take you as my witness: look at the Indian schools. The very name is a mockery. There is nothing Indian about them, except the colour of the students and their origin. The Indian language is not taught at all in their classes, and the Indian traditions even less. (Is there not such a school near your metropolis, white man who cares little, where the Mohawk children are forbidden to converse in their own language?)

I tell you this, as I tell you other things, in all grief, stripped of my very pride. There are bitter words to speak, harsh and joyless words.

Tell me, without their language, what remains of a people?

Deprived of their language and of their country, my people inspired no pity. Was remorse unknown among the conquerors? Nevertheless, it would have been praiseworthy to have allowed a third culture to flourish here, another race, a different language, capable of enriching the country with its traditions, with its wisdom and its intelligence.

We were told that we would have to adapt ourselves for our own good. The reserves were to be a transitional condition. The insidious indoctrination of the little ones, the procedure of endowing them with a language that was foreign to them, would permit, we were assured, our integration with the Canadian, with the white man.

To integrate — that means to absorb a people within oneself until nothing remains of them but a memory, and the odious deceits of the history textbooks.

The Indians — cruel, hypocritical and treacherous! Those beings who are considered inhuman only because they wished to defend their country against the White invasion.

In the white man's land, the cultivated areas, great stone monuments have been erected in the image of the defenders of Canadian soil: Dollard des Ormeaux, le Chevalier de Lévis, Salaberry, Montcalm... (I have little love for these men, and I name them without order and without care as to dates and victories...)

Why did they not erect monuments of the same granite and of the same dignity to the Indian chiefs who perished beneath the French muskets?

Were we of lesser courage, of lesser patriotism?

Why is it necessary, because of the colour of one's skin, to submit to a double burden, to suffer in double measure?

I stood up, a fool in my pride, and I read in the eyes of Lévesque, the superintendent of the reserve, a look of pity rather than of admiration, when I told him in my own language:

"I have come because I want my people to be free."

A look of pity only.

I waited a long time for him to reply. He paced the floor in front of me, making a circle of six strides around the low table, which brought him back to where he had started. This time, his expression was grave.

"It is very late," he said.

"It is not too late."

"As for myself, I preach patience," said Lévesque. I believe that I smiled at this.

"I am alone now," I said.

"I know; I was told."

"And to save my people, I can afford to sacrifice myself."

"You have the right," he said, "to think in your own way. But perhaps they do not want their freedom."

He touched my arm. I did not stiffen, because he was not a white man like the others. This was evident in his gestures and in the sound of his voice. He did not order me to do anything, and he treated me as an equal. More white men like this one would have been helpful in our history, and less of the others, such as those who wrote the treaties.

"Listen," said Lévesque, "I am trying to help you. I have just been transferred here, and it has taken some time to observe your people and to understand them. They are different from the Crees."

Did he want to teach me the superiority of my race?

"I have undertaken to help them. If you want, you can work with me. It is as you wish."

"I cannot discuss it with you," I said. "What I demand cannot be granted by you or by others like you. And, since I am assuming the leadership of the tribes, I become from that fact a chief. Tell the Great White Chief

65

at Ottawa that there is a chief here called Ashini, who wishes to hold conference with him."

Then I added, so that the issue would be completely clear between us:

"I am a man of little means. I have only the riches of the forests of Ungava. The Great White Chief has at his disposal swift airplanes, such as those that pass overhead frequently when I am up in my own territory. Tell him this: I shall await him on the Bersimis River, at the first large bend above the mouth, at the full moon of next month."

And I withdrew from his house, hastily.

I could not have remained near this man. I feared his respect, and I would perhaps have failed in my task by accepting some of the patience which he wished to inject, and which I did not want to have.

Our entire race has been dulled by patience. Using this virtue of the indecisive as a pretext, the Whites had caused my people to waver this way and that. So much so that today they no longer know any recipe other than this patience, which, for them, was nevertheless fatal.

I returned to the forest, and two hours'walk from the Indian village, I waited for a sign to be given me.

Chapter Seven

To what pressures was Tiernish subject-
ed, that he consented to come and find me in
the forest? What did they promise him, who
must have preferred the heat of his house,
to such a quest on a cold day?

Tiernish was trail-wise. He could move
straight towards his prey. It took him only
three hours to find me. Had it not been for
his indolence, what a magnificent inhabitant
of the forest that sluggish dullard would have
been!

"I have a message for you," he told me.

He carried the message inside his shirt, on
a piece of white paper. In Montagnais script,
Lévesque had written:

"What you ask is impossible. Come and
discuss it with me."

I waited no longer. This man could have
dismissed me. He could have humiliated me

in front of the whole village. He had chosen to discuss. This was a preliminary victory.

All was precisely as I had foreseen it. Even the written words were set out in the manner that I had imagined.

Would they ever know, these white men who took themselves for gods, that within the simple soul of a Montagnais like me there slept more insight and shrewdness than they could ever imagine?

Did he believe that I hoped to succeed by a simple request made from one man to another?

I had tracked the mink and trapped it; outwitted the fox, and lived solely on my own resources in a forest that is skilful in protecting its wild things. From this life I had acquired a knowledge which I could now place in the service of my resolution.

A knowledge and an art that vastly outstripped the orderly, inculcated thought processes of the white man.

Lévesque thought that he was playing a game of strategy: it did not even occur to him that I was the author of his strategy.

A good heart does not confer shrewdness.

69

It mattered little that he liked us, that he was on our side. He was a servant, and I intended to hold a conference with the master. And there was one thing I knew, amongst many others of great usefulness. The Great White Chief would not dare to lose face before his people.

And, obscure though I was, so far away and insignificant, I possessed one power, exactly that of touching the pride of this all-powerful person.

Without allowing the smile which illuminated me within to appear in my expression, and feigning to be misled by Lévesque, I went to see him.

This time, Lévesque received me in his office and offered me a seat. His appearance was grave, and his eyes were weary.

"I understand that you want to help your people," he told me. "I have been told that you are a proud man, and that you remain in the forest by choice. I am also told that you are the most competent woodsman of the Montagnais."

I nodded. The description of me was accurate.

"However, if you want to help your people, you will have to be more realistic. You see, I am not alone. I am in charge here only up to a certain point. In reality, I am an agent who is intermediate between all of you and the Department of Indian Affairs in Ottawa. Whenever possible, I take your part, and I have been able to have some of the policies changed which I have felt were harmful to my Indians."

(He had said "my Indians," and the tenderness in his voice did not escape me. I was satisfied that he had at heart something other than distrust or hatred. I felt his humility. But what could all that change? In his own words, and without my having to point it out to him, he was not really the master. The master who decided upon the fate of the people was down there in the town of Ottawa, in the house of the Great White Chief. And he was not anywhere else.)

"Tell the Great White Chief that I wish to hold conference with him."

Lévesque shrugged.

"Ashini, they say you are intelligent. And the way that you speak your language proves to me that you can reflect and think. But you are going about things the wrong way. The Great White Chief is, as you know, a busy man. He has many problems, because the Whites are more difficult to govern than the Indians. You know very well that he will never come away out here to Ungava to discuss with you."

Once again, I had foreseen every word of his reply. But he did not suspect this.

There remained only one more thing for me to say, one more point which I had undertaken to bring forth in this exchange.

"If he does not come, the Great White Chief will lose face, and will never be able to justify himself either to his own people or to mine."

Lévesque looked at me. He was a thin and nervous man, still young, who scrutinized the soul, and could read deeply into the substance of other beings.

This is a rare quality among the Whites. Few of them know how to look a man in the face.

"You are wasting your time," he said at last. "Even if I sent your message to the Prime

72

Minister of Canada, no one would take it seriously."

For the second time, I left him, and made my way back into the forest. But before parting from Lévesque, I repeated to him: "I will meet with your big chief on the bank of the Bersimis River, a day's travel by canoe above Betsiamits, in the middle of next month, when the moon is full. If your chief does not come, I will do what has to be done."

As there was a month to wait, I followed the portages as far as Lake Ouinokapau, where I had traps set, and could resume my daily life.

Chapter Eight

I remember the time when we used birch-bark.

The time when the echoes replied only in our own language. The time of the open trails, when men sat in meditation around the fires.

The time when the gestures of the women were slow and lingering, and the curve of their arms was like the curve of the great pendant willows.

In those times, there was never the smell of diesel oil in the woods.

And the only sound from the sky was the deep rumbling of the thunder on the horizon, on the warm summer evernings.

Then the birchbark was among us, like the blood in our veins and the deerskin on our shoulders.

It was simply a matter of removing as much bark as was needed from the birch tree.

And then we slipped along the soft, sweet waters in our canoes framed with seasoned hardwood, and covered with the supple bark of the birch.

And we ate at that time from bowls of birchbark which the women slung from forked branches in the evening, so that they hung just within the blue part of the flames.

And we sewed and we ran and we climbed and we drank, thanks to the birchbark.

Are there many Montagnais left today who remember the time of the bark? Those times of resinous smoke wreathing out across the surface of the lake, reaching out to welcome us on our return from the hunt?

(Yonder, on the dry point of a pine wood jutting out into the lake, the wigwams were white spots in the new evening.)

Do you remember, my father, how I carried the pail of birchbark from the transparent stream up to the hut where we stored the water? How small I was then, but that I believed in you? Do you remember, oh my father, in your Happy Hunting Ground where none of these things are important anymore,

do you remember the time of the bark, the
time of our felicity?

The time of the bow and arrow, and of the
spear made of wood hardened in the fire, armed
with a pointed stone?

The time when we were matchless hunters,
and the weapons of the beasts were equal to
our own?

Do you remember, father, and all you who
are no more, the blessed time of the birch?

In memory of all the living blood spilt,
initiator of our generations from one era to
the next, I have made a pact in the hope of
all good things, that for each of us will return
the time of the birchbark. Not in its former
reality, but in spirit, to impart to us the
rhythm of our daily lives.

The young Montagnais women must know
how to sing aloud from the heights of the
hills, so that their voices run along our skin
like fresh caresses.

Our young Montagnais women must take
their newborn child in both hands, and

offer it to the generous woodlands. the fish-laden waters, and the sun-filled sky, so that their appreciation of being the continuators of our blood be made known to the Manitous everywhere.

The hands of our men must touch the shining furs with respect and with honour, so that in every thicket new life will abound, and that tomorrow and in all future years the nourishing forest will be filled with riches.

The time of the birchbark renewed must be for all of us a return to a life of tranquility. Let there be no more despair, no more anguish, no human sound which is feared near our habitations. And let this time be the time of love renewed, because this is all man has; love was made for man and is his gift on earth.

Therefore, let the men know how to love, and the women even more so. In memory of the time of the birch, let the young girls be taught that there is no sound more godlike than the sound of love, no voice more penetrating and beautiful than the voice of love.

And to our men, the sweetness of their perpetuation serenely accomplished in the land of eternity.

I returned to my own hunting grounds at Lake Ouinokapau.

I resumed my usual life.

I do not mean that nothing had changed; but I returned to the life that I had always led. Neither my solitude, nor my project, nor the act which I must do in the time to come, could disturb this rhythm.

I slipped completely into my accustomed ways in this Ungava forest, in this special district that had become for me something between a place of habitation and a kingdom.

Here, the forest was composed of great black pines, of hardy firs, and of spruce; amongst the conifers, the hardwoods were sparsely commingled. A wood in which one could hunt at ease in the winter; a summer wood of the greatest richness. Honeysuckle, hawthorn, raspberries and wild blackberries abounded in the undergrowth, and all about, the swift-growing cedar thickets formed excellent hiding places for the wild hares. Fox, mink, fisher, and river otter also ran these pathways. On the far side of the lake there was a large and shallow bay. A colony of at least two hundred muskrats lived in it. On the bear trails one found also the spoor of the wolf; everywhere along the shores of the lake were moose tracks, and along the edges of the four clearings which bordered the lake, one could see the ravages of the deer.

Nests of songbirds were not rare, and these attracted the marten, whose fur is precious. Traces of partridge and of swamp hens showed wherever the damp soil was exposed.

Was this the way the world was when the Tshe first gave it to mankind? Had I found the perfect region wherein to establish our tribe? This country had been so generous to me. Is it so astonishing that I should wish to share it with others?

However, I did not seek to think too profoundly about my country. What was essential was to give my full attention to the realities of each day; for I had nothing further to hope for from this region, and could dream of no joys which it would bring me in the future.

I had chosen a destiny: nothing should move me to useless regrets.

When the month of May came, perhaps I would not hear the explosion of the ice giving way beneath the weight of the day. I would perhaps have finished my human span, and the long pilgrimages to the sterile land of the Montagnais deserters might no longer be my concern.

But against all logical foresight, did I not oppose an even greater fatalism?

I still set my traps where they would catch fur-bearing animals.

I did this simply, instinctively, as I had always done it, in the name of the continuity of life.

I believe that the only concession that I made to the new order of my destiny was to accomplish, upon my return, with some ceremony, my preparation of the first pelt.

There are rites to observe at each stage of life. When a child is born, the mother retreats into the forest in secret the night following its arrival. She carries the newborn infant to a hilltop. There, she suspends it from a tree; and all night she dances slowly around the tree. With one hand she takes away from the 'entshiskailnuit,' with slow and gentle gestures, all pain, all evil, all cruel destiny. Then, with the same gesture, she casts these dangers far away, to the bottom of the mountain, so that the spirits of the night may carry them off and master them.

And at the same time, she chants a rhythmic song, which she will keep secret until her son reaches manhood. When he has brought home to the wigwam his first kill of fresh meat, she will teach his song to him.

When I caught the first black mink in one of my traps, which was at the same time the first mink of that year, I thought it praiseworthy to perform a ceremonial because of it, to honour That which invisibly moves and governs beyond the skies, beyond my familiar world which I can touch and see.

It was our custom to give homage, and to carry out the rituals of propitiation.

The mink, which I had brought in stiffened with cold, became supple again when I laid it out by the heat of the fire.

Its dark sombre coat shone with bluish tints in the light of the flames. It was the finest catch that had been granted me for many years.

A symbol, perhaps, and the sign of a new time? The seal of promise?

I pierced the throat of the mink with the keen blade of my knife, and slit the skin slowly down the inside of the thighs.

This was the first step in skinning it. The second, I did not take immediately. Instead I held the beast that had died for me in my outstretched hands and lifted it above the things around me — the shelter of branches, the burning fire, the thickets of sprawling cedar. I held my spoil aloft in offering to the greatest of my gods, the Tshe Manitou; and then to the others — those of the forests and of the streams, those who guide the course of the waters, and those who bring forth the clouds in their pathways over the sky. Not one of those powers did I omit, not even those obscure and necessary ones who regulate the useful insects, those scavengers who keep the undergrowth clean by devouring carcasses, and will not tolerate the sullying of the area by the putrefaction of animals.

Homage to the Lords of Life (it is the Tshe Manitou himself who breathes the soul into the human being at the moment of birth), those divinities who assure our continued existence, and who establish and maintain under law the ordered course of nature; and to the humble gods also — the hagiography of my own religion — who have long held high the honour of the red race.

Holding the dead mink in my hands, I circled the fire in a dance which I had learned in my childhood; I made up a song, and in this song I pronounced the words of invocation.

For this is the way that our gods should be honoured, by making up one's own song from the depths of one's soul.

When I judged that I had given full homage, and when I felt the pleasure of the gods manifest itself within me, it was time for the second step.

I carefully removed the skin of the mink, separating the pelt from the layer of fat beneath with light, sure strokes. It took me a long time to finish this task, because it was important that this skin above all be of the highest quality, and that it bear not the slightest mark nor the least scratch.

I skinned the head also, and the tail. Stretched out on a frame, the skin showed the entire shape of the animal, and on the discarded carcass not one hair remained.

Thus is the task well and truly accomplished by one who has respect for his craft.

The black mink skin was perfect. By its colour, by the age of the creature, by the downy softness of the undercoat and the health of the guard hairs, I knew it was such a pelt as rarely comes to the counters of the factors.

All that night I fed my fire, so that heat and light might prevail. With a stone of the proper angle and roughness, which I kept in the bottom of a sock, I scraped off all the grease and flesh from the inside of the skin. Then I washed it thoroughly, and washed the fur also down to its depths.

I wrapped it up, and when I fell asleep with this pelt beneath my head, I knew it to be more than a symbol; I knew it to be indeed a sign from the gods accorded to my project.

Are there, then, in the invisible worlds which inspire the races, gods who can survive when their people are dying? It is true that paradise is for the elect only. But what will become of our gods if the Indians pay tribute to other gods, and none of us remain to invoke our Manitous in their own language?

In order to continue their work, will they not have to become only the gods of the pines and the birches, of the beasts and of the hundred thousand lakes, as they had been in ancient times?

I was sure now of being not only their free agent who was concerned with new beginnings, but also their redeemer amongst my little band.

I could not ask for more.

Chapter Nine

Many hundreds, or many thousands, of years before, my country was inhabited only by the beasts. Man had not yet come there. There was no echo of the sound of man in the woods, and if the beasts had enemies, they were not this unpredictable, hypocritical and inventive biped who came later.

The absence of man did not mean that the forest was safe for the creatures living in it. Each species had its destined pattern of life just the same.

But the wolves united into packs in a year of scarcity when the easy prey had been decimated too rapidly.

The first wolf pack, according to our legends, was organized in the area of Lake Kakush, the Lake of the Porcupines. Huala, a very skilful and intelligent young wolf, saw one day a huge moose, which was drinking along the shore. Huala was hungry, and he knew that the other wolves in the vicinity were hungry too. Crouching in a thicket, he savoured the odour of the moose for a long time, observed the beast, and estimated his chances.

But Huala was intelligent, and his courage was tempered with wisdom. Seeing that the moose was going to depart, he suddenly had the idea of calling other wolves to his aid. But how to do it? Huala knew only one call which would carry far enough, that of the male calling the female, the mating call, which would surely astonish all the she-wolves within hearing, and which would intrigue the males.

The moose snorted, and in a few moments it started away. Huala knew that he was powerless to attack the enormous beast, which could crush him with the blows of its hooves. And if the wolf launched himself at the carotid artery of the beast, getting a grip and holding on, the animal, bleeding to death, in tossing its great and powerful neck, could knock Huala senseless against the stones and the trunks of the trees.

No — he must have help. All of the wolves would have to come. In desperation, Huala started to howl. The moose bounded towards the forest, but Huala, still howling, pursued it.

The forest at first knew only an astonished silence at the howling of the wolf. All the animals kept still, listening to the call that no one expected to hear until some day in October.

Then, far away, a female responded. Huala recognized the voice of the young she-wolf, a rather timid voice which questioned more than it replied.

But this first reponse, in a ritual that was to become traditional, provoked the curiosity of the other wolves in the area. Soon, the voices of males rang out in interrogation. And suddenly it was a concert. From every ridge, and from the depths of the valley, some thirty wolves entered into conversation with Huala. All this time, the young wolf continued in pursuit of the moose.

Did the she-wolf understand what Huala wanted ? Did instinct prompt the wolves ? The legend does not tell us. We are sure of only one thing — the wolves and she-wolves came to Huala's call. Soon, they were running at his side, and there was not one wolf but an entire pack harassing the great moose, a pack that was famished and furious, and who pressed on henceforth in silence.

There was not a sound in the whole forest but the laboured gasps of the tall creature, whose wind was failing, and behind him, the padding, swift paws of the wolves, an agile, compact and implacable mass from which issued from time to time a brief growling or snapping, the route orders thrown out by Huala, who had taken the leadership of the pack.

They caught the moose at the edge of another lake. The entire pack hurled themselves at the kill. A ravenous feast began, and when their hunger was sated, only some scattered bones remained.

After the pack had slept, Huala communicated these thoughts to them:

"You were hungry; I called you; and you ate. If you want, it can be this way every night."

The she-wolves, admiring, fixed their eyes upon this young and confident male who displayed such fine assurance. The wolves who were older than Huala, or less audacious, held council. There were dissident voices. One old wolf retired from this new pack and went his way, solitary and ill-tempered.

"I will be your chief," said Huala, "until the day when I can no longer find game for you."

Thus was born the first pack.

Huala spent a day examining animal trails and observing the movements of the animals. At nightfall, he went up to the top of a hill and sounded his clear rallying call. And from every brake and every hollow in the surrounding district poured forth the replies. Within half an hour, the pack had gathered. Huala instructed the beasts as to the nature of the prey, and the silent hunt began.

By the time the first men with copper-coloured skin appeared in the forest, other wolf packs had formed, and there were hundreds of packs hunting the Far North. But there followed also packs of men, a young man at their head, just as among the wolves. And the animals of the forests cowered and hid away, in order not to be killed, and questioned which pack was the more cruel, the wolf pack or the human.

And so it was because of both the wolves and the men that the animals of the forest learned to be more crafty. Until then, they had no enemies other than those ordained by the woodland gods. Now a more formidable enemy than the wolves appeared: Man —skilful, cunning, inventive, forbidding.

The enemy of all the animals, man fed himself on the greater beasts, the hares, and even the porcupines. He slaughtered mink, muskrat, otter, marten, fisher, beaver, wildcat, weasel, lynx and fox, for their fur. He killed wolves, with the claim of self-defence from their attacks. He slew birds, massacred squirrels, seized fish from the lakes and rivers, stole the wax and honey from the bees, snatched the bear cub from its mother, and demolished the dams built by the beaver.

And man was treacherous. He would kill a moose, cut it up into a hundred scraps of flesh, and sow them all along the edges of the lake. And when the fox and the marten, the mink and the fisher came to feast, he trans-

91

fixed the poor beasts with arrows, or strangled them with collars of supple "babiche" slung insidiously in their pathways.

Hundreds of years later — or thousands — still other men came, men of white skin who carried thunder in their hands, and who set out, not supple collars, but frightful traps of metal which tore the flesh.

From this petty warfare was born the great craftiness of the animals of the forest. From one generation to the next, new instincts were transmitted. And the animals succeeded in foiling men more often than men succeeded in tracking them.

The animals learned the need for silence. They found places to hide underground for hours. When pursued by too many enemies at one time, they did not always allow themselves to be decimated, but emigrated to more peaceful regions, abandoning entire territories.

The day came when the animal dealt with man on more equal terms. It was no longer the law of the strongest, but the law of the most cunning: a game of skill between them.

Perhaps it took a thousand years, but whereas in former times the fox walked confidently with tail curled towards the sky, and stalked freely through the woods, he learned little by little to glide silently, his tail between his legs; he learned to leap upon his prey and take flight immediately. If the slightest taint of man were on the wind, the fox would disappear. Formerly, he had never known flight; who can catch him now when he flees?

And it was this way for each animal.

Their gait, their habitations, the time when they hunted, and even the nature of their prey changed.

But above all, they received an apprenticeship in guile, and the habit of cunning by its continuous usage.

And so, at first because of the wolves, and then because of Man (and both the wolf and the man hunt in packs, a dual danger for every beast) all the wildlife of the woods became adapted to these new ways.

Could I not myself find inspiration equally in Huala, the inventor of the pack, and in those ancient expeditions when the man-leader led his own pack to the kill?

To reassemble the Montagnais. To be a man-wolf, a man-leader — temporarily, as may be — gathering his people for their needs, placing himself at their head, and leading them free at last, into this country which I would guarantee to them?

For a month I lived there, hunting, trapping and pondering. The elements of my life formed a well-knit whole, as it should be with a man who lives in the forest and from the forest, if he wishes to obtain from it the utmost good.

I meditated, because this was necessary. I mastered my future, and determined it.

And more — I hoped.

And when I arrived at the meeting place on the Bersimis, where I knew very well I would not find the Great White Chief, and he was not there, I wept, nevertheless, for my weariness was great, and my age weighed heavily upon me, and I would so much have wished to have been wrong, and to have received in good grace what I now knew must be wrested from the Whites.

Chapter Ten

The bend in the river was long and wide, and smooth, too, smooth enough to land an airplane on, and its broad surface was frozen solid. When I arrived, there was nothing there.

I waited for four days, but no airplane bearing the Great White Chief appeared in the sky.

There was not even a messenger to bring excuses.

I had invited a chief to meet with me, but he had not had the courtesy of chiefs.

And this is why warfare continues on earth, because the representatives of peoples do not learn the code of behaviour and will not respect the customs of their brothers of other races.

I have never seen it decreed in the skies that I, a Redskin, am created inferior to the white prime minister who rules in Ottawa.

He feels the cold as I do; he feels hunger as I do. He is moved by the same griefs, and any bullet entering his body will tear his flesh as much as it would my own.

The wind will blow over him as it does over me, and water will drown him as it drowns the Montagnais. The same mosquitoes harass him, and our women are mated in the same way.

His house is warmer than mine, perhaps, and his fortune is great; but my riches are my country, and my country is immense. This man can, if he wants to, load up a great ship and sail around the world; but could he, as I do, jump the rapids at will in a canoe of birchbark?

Weigh us in an honest balance; weigh us justly. In skin, in blood, in what is good and what is not good in us, organ for organ, muscle for muscle, is he different from me?

Nourished more finely than I am, he would perhaps be eaten with greater relish by some wolf who is a gourmet among his kind. But I do not see in that an enviable superiority.

At the end of four days, I moved closer to the reserve. I would return to my own territory only after my task had been accomplished, and its outcome became apparent, whatever results these were to be.

Between Bersimis and the Manicouagan, there is a rapid which runs along the plateau behind the road. It turns obliquely, as if intending to join the Bersimis, and then bends back again towards the sea. In this right angle is an open wood of tall pines and large willows. Near the rapid, difficult of access and surrounded by dense brush, is a clearing as large as three teepees. It is sandy, and rarely covered with snow in the winter.

This clearing has an autumnal quietude. And being thus, it is a sort of retreat, hidden and welcoming.

It was there that I constructed my shelter. I was sure that no one could find me there. If I covered my tracks when going and coming, even the Montagnais of the reserve would be unable to trail me.

Maybe Tiernish would be skilful enough, but I was certain that he would not agree a second time to exert the effort.

Pikal? The others? Who knows? In how many of them still remained the science of the forest, and that condition of awareness essential to survival?

Therefore I was at home in my narrow clearing. From there I could carry out the steps of my programme.

Now the last phase of my plan could be set into motion, the concluding steps, the irreversible undertaking.

(How had I brought myself to this point? Certainly I felt hesitant at times, even fearful. Sometimes even a kind of panic. Indeed, I feel the same anguish as a white man, and that I may receive it differently or disguise it better does not alter the fact. I am a man among men — which is perhaps the most terrible of condemnations. Had I been an inferior creature, a pariah existing beneath the level of the human race, I would have felt neither pride nor anguish, neither revulsion nor panic.)

I remember that once, when I was thirty years old, after an incredible portage and endless climbing, I found myself on the heights and summits of Mount Taurus. We were three in the expedition — a cousin, another Montagnais unrelated to us, and I.

For two days we lived on the escarpments of the mountain, a series of granite faces separated by narrow ledges where we made our fires and slept.

If I should tell you what I felt that evening near the reserve, when I was about to conquer the world, there comes to mind the image of a single stone which I dislodged with my foot thirty years before, on the flank of that precipitous mountain.

Only one stone on that morning ricocheted down the sharp edge of the slope. It dislodged two others, which continued to roll down with the first. There followed another ten, then twenty, and the number became so great that I ceased to count them.

And it became an avalanche, became a scourge which gouged out the whole flank of the mountain, uprooting trees, effacing hillocks, and ploughing out ravines.

When its thunder died away, and only a little smoke chased by the wind remained in the blue air, the country at the foot of the mountain was completely changed.

One stone, as large as my fist, dislodged by my clumsy foot.

So little.

Tshe Manitou, was I marked out for two such cataclysms separated by thirty years of time?

But I was no longer clumsy, believe me. I remembered that stone, and if I unleashed so much as the power of my fist so that an avalanche would be started in the country of the white man, it was premeditated and calculated.

In spite of my panic.

In spite of the anguish.

In spite of every caution of false prudence within me, the protesting instinct of survival which warned me of dangers to come.

Who, better than I, could know the dangers? Who else had discounted the effects?

In his far-away town, and because of me, the Great White Chief would lose face.

I had no other intention. My every gesture, every decision, each new step revolved around this absolute fact. He would lose face.

And I, I might die.

If necessary, I consented to my own death, if through it my people might be reborn.

If it were necessary.

Stretched out in my shelter, for two days I communed with myself. I banked up my fire until it was only embers and the least possible smoke escaped from it.

No one knew that I was there, and it did not suit my purpose that they find out too soon.

As for myself, was I really aware of inhabiting a precise location on earth? It seemed to me that I inhabited time and that I had the stars for guides, rather than the undulations of the mountains, the pathways of the rivers, and the indentations of the lakes.

My country belonged, so to speak, more to a dream than to geography. There was grandeur in what I was doing — I could no longer doubt this.

A sequence of actions, simple but definite. And in the end, the inescapable conclusion.

Truly man reaches the feet of the gods, when he masters his own nature.

Great White Chief, have you guessed for a single instant the force against which you are measured?

For those in the great cities think they are knowledgeable. But what is their knowledge as compared to mine?

It would not take many days to find out how to live in the subjugated regions. Everything there is conceived in such a way that a man need know nothing, fear nothing, imagine nothing. Everything is put within his reach, and the most limited of beings could not go astray in such a place.

Whereas here in my forest, white man, can you imagine what I have to know?

What I must remember, fear, utilize and foresee; what skills I must possess?

To live in the forest, I must engrave in my memory every hole and hollow, every promontory and elevation. The smallest swamp, ravine or undulation, and every slope and curve of a mountain must be familiar to me. Only in this way can I make the free lands my home. Thus I can recognize the habitations of the animals, the areas good for trapping, the certainty of a campsite, the presence of creeks or rapids, of springs and rivers. By its colour as well as by its shape, this paler green indicates poplar and birch, succulent woods wherein the large animals have their stamping-grounds. In the stony areas are the caverns and grottoes where the bear and the wolf make their lairs. The mossy uplands, where the conifers grow, is the country of hare and squirrel. The regions of soft, deep soil, covered with tall grasses and sweet shrubbery are good places for quail, partridge, woodcock, pheasant, and, among the animals, the porcupine. The groves of hardwood, such as are called mixed forest, with their streams and humid earth (the soil elsewhere is dry and yellow), their varied perfumes, their thickets and sprawling cedars, hawthorn trees, eglantine, with bayberry shrubs too, wild cherries and wild raspberries, are the places for bear, mink, otter, fisher and small marten.

I have known all these things from infancy. That which was the summer forest, but which was also the winter forest, in which the disposition and abundance of the snow was controlled with precision by the diverse location and type of the trees. And of this forest

I had to know not only what lives and grows, but also what lies upon the ground, the snow being not the least of this.

What guides me above all is the colour of the snow. To the uninitiated, all snow is similar, or he believes it to be so. Few novices would see the shades of difference in the forest.

In mid-winter, the snow is hard and white — so white that with the least sunshine it is so dazzling that it could blind one. When March comes, and snow storms are less frequent, the white carpet becomes even harder, and forms a final crust which is thick and solid. Then here and there under the trees the snow shows patches of dust and needles which have fallen from the branches when the wind has stirred them and rubbed them together. There are also traces of the excrement of animals, and the urine of bear or deer yellows the whiteness in many places.

But when the end of April comes, or the beginning of May, where the great forests of the North lie, so far that the winters stay for a much longer time, then the heat from the south mounts north through and along the earth. Here and there, the snow takes on a hue which is neither white nor grey. It has a washed-out appearance. Sometimes one can perceive beneath the white a sort of grey-black, sombre cast which appears because of the increasing transparency of the crust. And it is there where treachery is hidden.

To set foot on such snow means to sink into it down to the bottom, a bottom which is liquid, clutching, possessing almost the qualities of quicksand.

And what if there were beneath the snow a ravine or crevasse, instead of solid ground?

Anyone who fell into such a trap and could not get out would be seized with panic. Alone in the wilderness, his cries would not be heard. The moving, crumbling mass would suck him in, and he would die there like an animal.

These are just a few of the understandings that I have had to acquire, white man, during the course of my life. They were acquired by lengthy experience, and called for the constant exercise of my judgment.

Tell me, is there in your own life, the life of your cities and cultivated lands, of well-made roads, sign posts and landmarks, the need of skills equal to mine?

Why do you think I am inferior to you, you who would perish within three days in my forest?

Show me the allure of your civilization, intruder, of the atoms you split, of the incredible energy which you abuse, of your unequal laws! Compare your values and mine!

You think you have power? A single bolt of lightning when it strikes a great pine is more powerful than all your laboured machines.

The force of a hurricane, which can devastate twenty counties, is it not more than comparable to your murderous bombs?

And tell me if your science can create a single black pine, even a single flower, or can colour the sunset or create the rich aroma of the noon in May...?

Chapter Eleven

The fifth day of my presence on the out-skirts of the village, I pierced a vein in my arm and traced the first of my messages on a piece of birchbark with my blood:

The Great White Chief did not come. I will await him again at the same place in six days. If he does not come, he will lose face.

I waited for nightfall; then I slipped towards the house of the white man on the reserve.

I, Ashini of the northern forests, had no-thing to fear from the Montagnais of Bet-siamits. They were all asleep, and a catas-trophe could have come without their being aware of its approach.

Not one house had its eyes open. The village was a silent and shapeless mass which I could no longer recognize.

But the sea beat rhythmically upon the shore. It was alive, and brought me back to myself. Why were they all asleep?

The hearing and the sense of smell of the Montagnais are very sensitive; they enable him to recognize and interpret arrivals and movements at a great distance.

The eye of the Montagnais closes only halfway, when he lives according to the laws of his race.

And yet I was going through this village like a ram amongst his flock. To what end, this paternalism of the white man, which plunged the people of the great wilderness into sleep so heavy that one could cut their throats without fear... ?

I could have entered any one of these houses at Betsiamits, I could have come and gone at will, killed or stolen. And these are bitter truths, truths which strike to the heart of all resolutions.

To salvage, to rebuild, to remould and regenerate! To lead them from this nothingness which was their present lot, to unearth their past, to multiply these people a hundredfold, to magnify them, to incarnate in them...

The village of Betsiamits was laid out far from the paved road. There is a street which runs along, joins another street, then widens out and forks; then the church, the priest's house, the school, and the buildings needful to a White administration; and at the end of all that, and facing it, the sea.

(You know, I speak little of the sea because it has never been one of our native elements; we have derived neither pleasure nor utility from it. We have never undertaken to build boats or to fish from its wide expanse, as the white man does. A few of us have hunted the narwhale with rifles out on the ice flows; but this was when serving the White, toiling to earn a few pennies.

There are no beautiful words in my language with which to describe the sea, or to sing about it. I have often dreamed that we could have found there an immensity which would have been good for us; but nevertheless we re-treated from it.

Certainly, our tribes have often camped on its shores, mostly at the mouths of the rivers because of the salmon which come up to spawn. And there were also fruits near the sea, and open ground for those among us who were wearied of the encumbering forest.

But we have never travelled the sea as the white man travels it. Perhaps this is because it does not offer us any point of reference, and we need to scrutinize the outline of the horizon to feel confident of ourselves.

What would I do in a fog at sea?

Or how would I find my position on days which were overcast and grey, and the horizon merged with the water? How would I retrace my path? For the crest of a wave is not the strong summit of a mountain.

The sea, which could have been our friend, remained a kind of silent enemy...)

I observed the life of the reserve all that day, from my lookout.

I think that the white man was preoccupied, because I saw him going around knocking on many doors. On the door, in any case, of Pikal.

Was he looking for support?

Or was he trying to learn something about me which would give him the means of defeating me? He liked the Indians, but which ones? Docile Indians or rebel Indians?

Or, on the other hand, would he be my ally, and participate in my project?

On the black wires running out of the reserve along pillars right into the civilized part of the country, what was being said that morning? What secret harangues were beating forth into the distance on these mysterious tom-toms?

I had the knowledge of the earth, and none other. I could not know what discussions had taken place between the Whites at a distance and the one close at hand, who was so busy at this time.

I saw also that the priests of the white religion were very busy in their turn. One of them conferred for quite a while with Tiernish on the pow-wow grounds behind the church. But Tiernish constantly shook his head, which somewhat reassured me.

He was the only one who still could sniff out a trail along the ground. To have found me would have been only a game... If it was a matter of tracking me, what fate willed that he refuse?

The snowmobile carrying the mail came through the trail and passed near enough for me to touch it; then it veered obliquely onto the road into the reserve. Would my message be put in a sack, with Ottawa as its destination? Would it be given there to the Great Chief?

And what would the Great White Chief do then?

I felt a hope invade my heart, foolish and magnificent. What if he agreed to a conference? What if I could make him understand the good that I wished to accomplish?

What if he came here, and saw the beaten eyes of the women, the sorry children, the motionless men? If he realized all of a sudden that my request would not only return their honour to the Montagnais, but would give Canada as a whole a new people to add to the others, a new richness, a new knowledge, and the return of a great wisdom?

In my dream, I saw already the participation of our chiefs in the regular conferences of the white man, bringing the gift of our traditions.

"Trench out this great canal if you will, but in doing so, respect the watershed which will irrigate your regions of flax and clover. Carry

112

out this matter as far as you wish, but in such a way that the crops which the people need may flourish."

Nothing — so little...

"This is not the time to undertake the extension of your influence. The raising of troops is forbidden by the signs in the sky. And there is no combat more warlike than the combat of man against nature. The struggles of man against man are the gymnastics of insects, and none of the gods are concerned with these. But push back the mountains or harness the waters, and your war with the Manitous who have dominion over earth and water becomes terrible. Wait for this work until the Tshe Manitou, who is above all the gods, gives you a sign of his will in the heavens..."

Certainly, the white man would laugh at this.

The methodical Englishman and the scoffing French Canadian would mock the importunity of our chiefs. But when a hundred such predictions had been confirmed and their wisdom proven, would our chiefs not be acclaimed and quickly raised to the level of leaders?

It was a dream.

After a delay of six days, and in spite of the bustling activity on the reserve, once again neither the Great Chief nor his delegate came to the meeting place on the Bersimis River. And then the third step of my plan remained to be taken.

Chapter Twelve

Kaya, the wolf, collapsed against the log and lay there, prone, waiting. But he did not wish to die. He tried to fight the pain that plunged within him, to drive it out and recover his strength. When staggering through a thicket, he had chewed some leaves whose effects he knew to be beneficial, but the pain had not disappeared. On a mound where there was bare soil and the earth was humid, he had rolled about in order to cover the wound with humus. With his saliva-laden tongue he soaked the humus, so that it became muddy and worked up into the gaping lips of the tear in his flank.

Motionless now, well sheltered, and hidden from view, he could wait for the pain to heal. His mother, a great she-wolf from Mishikamau, had taught him these things when he was young.

The time of his youth was long ago. He had spent years in his animal vocations. Kaya had been a force in the pack. When he howled, fifty voices replied from the four corners of the horizon. Had he ever counted his pack? How many young females had been attracted to his pack from others, fascinated by his personal odour? The odour of mastery, the effluent of the strength of his muscles, of his agility and his cunning?

Who better than he could lead the pack to the blood?

Who?

The other...?

Filled with pain, combating death with all his force, Kaya lay with his muzzle stretched out flat between his paws, remembering the months just past.

The other...

The other was the young Kimla. A stranger among them, an intruder from the Cahonga, loud-voiced and disrespectful. He would bound out of a thicket and carry off the prey every time. Had Kimla ever been seen with an empty mouth?

116

Kaya against Kimla. But it took strength. And it took the respect of the pack. Would they be concerned about him? Would some young female come sniffing through the bushes, to discover Kaya? His odour had not attracted the females for a long time. It was to Kimla that they went.

Kaya stiffened. He refused to think about those things. It was admitting defeat without combat. Kimla was only a scatterbrain who had the good luck to live in a forest which was full of game. What if he had lived in the old times when the forest was deserted and one had to hunt for two days to find a deer . . . ? When there were not even enough rats and moles to feed the wolf-cubs whimpering in their lairs?

The old wolf stirred, and the pain gripped him. He breathed harder, but did not whimper. One had to be silent, still. Secrecy was necessary.

Secrecy was needed above all. He did not want the pack to know where he was. Although perhaps this would give Kimla the liberty he desired, the chance to claim the leadership and to anchor his position at the head of the pack.

Kaya could not present himself to the pack with this wound. A female would come to sniff his flank, and would she not go off and relate how a mink had attacked him? How he, Kaya, head of the pack, while walking down a trail, had stupidly allowed a mink to leap upon his flank and bite him? And that this mink, a young and strong one, had almost got the better of the old wolf, who was no longer as competent and agile as before?

The pack would learn of Kaya's weakness, and the young males, with Kimla at their head, would throw themselves upon him and devour him.

A weasel appeared close by, thrusting its head over the shrubs. It observed the grey mass of the old wolf, considered the reason for his presence there, casting its eyes over Kaya and along his flank. It did not even seem nervous; at least, the panting breath of the old wolf did not frighten it. It darted up to him swiftly, coming within reach of his paw. Kaya, on his guard, struck out with his claws. But the old wolf missed. The small beast dodged the blow with one jump to the side, and sprang upon the bleeding wound.

Kaya, despairing, began to howl. What was happening to him? Why this atrocious panic, this terror in his bowels? He howled, calling the pack to his rescue, suddenly indifferent to whatever they might think. Only one thing mattered, to get rid of this animal and remove this danger! It was capable of leaping at his throat, of cutting his carotid artery with its piercing teeth, And what could he do against it?

The old wolf called and called, but the pack did not come. Only Kimla came, and stood there a moment, surveying the scene. His mouth was open, and a sort of grin revealed his fangs. Victory had come to him swiftly and well, the pack would be his, and Kaya would never contest it again.

He leapt upon the old wolf. The weasel fled. In the frozen herbage, and then out on the snow, and then in the glazed thickets once more, the two wolves held battle.

(Do you understand a little why I tell you the story of Kimla, the victorious wolf? And that of Kaya, the old wolf rejected by the pack?

119

Will you believe that I, who have not hidden the length of my years from you, see in Kaya my own image?

Go back a little in your thoughts, and think that the old wolf is I. I, who am, so to speak, rejected by the pack. I, who lick my gaping wounds to ease this pain within which has become my life.

And Kimla... Kimla the young, the audacious, the powerful, who sweeps aside everything, who repulses brutally anything that bars his way — who is he? Do I have to tell you?

Who is young in this country, and strong, and cruel? Who is intransigent, and creates brutal obstacles?

Your incessant, petty warfare, white man, is of the same pattern as the harassment of the old Kaya by the young wolf Kimla. And the pack is in the rear, attentive, holding its breath, cruel with the cruel, capable of compassion only if its masters have pity. Capable of devouring, also, if they are given sufficient reason.

The cruel Indian was soon overcome and we were able to bring about the evangelization of the tribes.

Show me a god who looks kindly upon me as well as upon you. And let him require kindness of you also, white man.

Is this so much to ask?

Kaya, unsuspecting, allowed Kimla to enter the territory of the pack. From that instant, it was all up with the old Kaya.

Should we not have pushed the Whites back into the sea from the very first day? Should we not have set up ambushes, blockaded the rivers, dried up the fresh springs and fouled the trails?)

Kimla bounded upon Kaya. On that day, in that place, and for longer than one would have thought possible, two wolves battled until the death of one of them.

It was Kimla who survived.

In my terrible anger, I could have run mad, blindly striking great blows at the trees, trampling the plants, and howling like an enraged beast. And these futile and useless gestures, without consequence and without reason, could have exorcised the resentment

121

mounting within me, coming from a hundred past generations.

And, contrary to Kaya, I could have shaken off my age and my weariness, I could have aroused the living force of my tribes and launched them to the assault of all the Kim-las.

I would have wished to; but I had learned long ago that to accomplish anything, I would have to restrain my blows, silence my voice, appease the tribes, assume the impenetrable countenance of my ancestors, and offer the White only the combat of ruse and astuteness.

In what strange pathways were my feet ensnared ?

Chapter Thirteen

Six more days of that time had run out, and
nothing had happened, and no one had come.
At the conjunction of the equinoxes, when the
great north-westerly winds blow, storms
might well confound the sky; but no star takes
note of them.

I, Ashini, a descendant of the eternal race,
recognized in the end that the last true
Montagnais seed in the country was in me.

The second message was written in the same
blood and delivered in the same fashion, but
later at night. So late that the pale rays of
dawn already caressed the sea in the east.
And the reserve, in its grey silence, with the
houses all in rows, gave the impression of a
strange cemetery. The cemetery of a nation,
marked with symbolic headstones.

Perhaps, indeed, it was the truth, this death
of Pikal, of Tiernish, of all the others, of each

woman and of each man, the issue of our former greatness. And that in the morning there would be none left living to awaken, but only the phantoms of a people who had disappeared.

In that heavy and moonless night, in which lethargy and stillness prevailed, I nailed the second message to the door of Lévesque:

If the Great White Chief does not come to discuss the liberation of my people within three days, he will lose face.

Is there a man of honour, with the seed of his perpetuation in him, who would accept such a profound insult to his pride and to his dignity? Who can lose face without flinching?

From the depths of my savage country, I, Ashini, was able to cast an insult at the prime minister of Canada. He would never recover from it, because it is the sacred duty of chiefs to occupy the highest summits of honour. That is the first condition of those to whom the gods have accorded the destiny of power. No one may rule who has lost face, for henceforth their chieftainship would be a deceit.

For three days I slept. A long and sinister lassitude overcame me; the need, one might have said, of finding refuge in the worlds of dreams, or perhaps in my own reality, which awaited me.

Like an animal that rolls itself up into a ball and hibernates, only half alive.

Dreams came to me.

I was borne into the ancient lands where the Montagnais occupied the high ridges and the promontories. And the assembled tribes sang a great chant of love of the earth, as in one voice, and of the gifts of the gods.

How can I tell you of these dreams? They were a continuous train of images, a great unfolding panorama which I contemplated from afar, in which I participated without moving, included, yet held apart.

I was one of them. (I was singing with them, and I was happy with the same joy as they.) But nevertheless I knew that I was only a defeated Montagnais asleep beneath a shelter of boughs.

A man separated himself from the others, climbed down the valleys, and came to touch my shoulder.

125

"What is your name?" he asked me.

"Ashini, and I live on Lake Ouinokapau."

"I also am named Ashini," said the other, who had descended to the gates of the Lower World.

He reopened the wounds on my arm, and took some of my blood, which he touched with his finger, and tasted.

"This blood is pure and worthy," he said. "It has the savour of sacrifice."

I awoke, and understood that a message had been given to me. From the depths of the Land of Good Hunting, the gods had consecrated my work.

At the dawn of the following days, all blood spilt would bring honour and perpetuity. I was no longer alone. I would never be alone again. I had found my immortal soul, and would live in this sacred companionship. The names of my elder son or of my younger son were no longer on my lips and I could forget the name of the daughter who had fled. I would now inhabit the final encampment, the land of the great-hearted, of the chosen ones.

"This blood is pure and worthy. It has the savour of sacrifice..."

Henceforth, there was nothing further that could happen. The road had been travelled to the end; the work had come to term. I had set up a "teepee" which would be indestructible.

Three days had passed. The Great White Chief had not come. I lanced my arm once more, and collected the blood in a bark vessel.

At dawn on the following day, I delivered this last message. If my coming had been awaited in the darkness of the night, the waiting must have been wearisome, because now I came when the sun was rising in the east, when all possible watchers would have gone to sleep.

When Lévesque found the message, he would read in it the last human words that I would write:

Now the Great White Chief will lose face, and the entire country will be shaken. Those who will watch the symbol of their down-fall tomorrow, will see me in all my force.

127

Chapter Fourteen

A road descends from the Metropolis and skirts the Indian village of Betsiamits.

The Whites have constructed a thin steel bridge, an enormous and ugly mass, which links the steep banks of the Bersimis.

Where the road leaves the bridge and enters the territories conceded to us, there is a post at the edge of the road on which is nailed an odious sign. It reads:

BERSIMIS RIVER INDIAN RESERVE

I have often contemplated this boundary mark with horror. There it stood in all its power, this symbol of segregation. The intangible barbed wire fence, the impediment, the constraint.

And it was there, in plain view, in the breath of the icy wind and in the light of the winter morning, that I would fulfil my destiny and assure that of my people.

My voice had not been heard, the voice of a man crying in his wilderness. But other voices would be heard: the horrified voices of the just, for once the stronger, massed for once, and demanding lawful justice.

When I came to the sign post, the surroundings were deserted. More deserted, it seemed to me, than they had ever been.

What were the fallen Montagnais dreaming in their soft beds?

Beneath how many of those roofs had the act of continuation been performed that night in the Indian village of Betsiamits, whose fruit would be, unknown to them at this time, the firstborn of the new and free Montagnais race?

Would they ever know that they owed their new blood to me, be it only in the indistinct memory of a rebellious school boy?

Would my name be sweetness and pride to them?

From the top of the white wooden post, I slung the straps of the harness I had made for the purpose.

Hanging there, my feet touching the ground only with difficulty, I swung in the winds of the morning.

Then, with my knife, I cut the artery of my right wrist, and immediately afterwards, that of my left wrist.

In the pale morning, in one swift wave, all the life flowed out of my body.

But I did not know while I was dying by inches, hanging from my new cross, that not one of the messages had been sent to the Great White Chief.

Nor that on the official death certificate the final insult would be inscribed:

Ashini, Montagnais, 63 years, suicide in a moment of mental alienation.

Epilogue

There followed a profound darkness, from which I emerged into an immense illumination.

I live now at the side of the beneficent Tshe Manitou, in the Land of Good Hunting, beyond the gates of life.

I have found there those of my own who died before. I have the favour of all the Manitous under the Tshe Manitou, the One divisible and infinite, for having undertaken, in the name of my tribes, a combat that was heroic and without issue.

Here I have learned all the events of all the lives which were dear to me. The anguish of my wife, the remorse of my son, who was almost a deserter when the bullet of the white man withdrew his life. And the painful steps of the death of my elder son when he perished by the lonely mountain.

131

But I know now also the joys they had, and the secret desire consuming the heart of my living daughter, that of finding once more our ancient happiness.

And I am in possession of all sciences.

Those of the interior design of the forest, those of the riverbanks, of the waters, of the mountains and of the valleys.

All the words, innumerable and subtle, which were ever created in my language, and the rhythm of their expression, so that henceforth they come to me without effort, and I can trace upon birchbark, in my inexhaustible blood, the pages of this book.

I see also the enterprises of the Whites in my country. And I see the misery of the Indians. And I measure to their exact size the powers of the Whites, their towns, their industries, their dams, and the roads with which they already shred my forest.

And I no longer doubt now that to exchange their rags for shining leather jackets, to live in houses where no winter wind will ever enter, the Montagnais must relinquish forever what they have been, and what they could be.

It is not a matter of the Whites imposing these things. The Whites do not even dream of discussing it, so much do their ways appear to them to be logical and good.

As in former times they offered us beads and trinkets in exchange for prime furs, today they offer my people neon lights, paved streets, and suits of terylene.

And the misfortune is that my people do not recognize the folly of these markets for dupes.

They do not know what they are giving in exchange, because nobody has told them, and there are no words in the white man's language to describe riches which are beyond measure.

Neither the people of the reserve, nor even the Whites of the towns, have yet learned why I died. And the Great White Chief did not lose face.

He never even received my messages.

And so today I write this book of blood. There is no need for it to be read. In my world beyond, I can so work that each one of the words of my language, such as I have inscribed it on these pieces of bark, will find an echo in one of my descendants, and that, for the just return of all remorse, that son will transmit this tale.

But my people are so small, and the other people so great, that this story will produce no more effect than an arrowhead chipped out of flint, silent in the showcase of a museum, for the delight of the curious, who, however, will have no understanding of its ancient importance.

Printed by
Les Éditions Marquis Ltée
Montmagny